The Mastermind: Introducing Lady Einstein

A Short Story
By

Ravoshia Whaley

This is a work of fiction. Similarities to real people, places, or events are entirely coincidental.

THE MASTERMIND: INTRODUCING LADY EINSTEIN

First edition. July 11, 2024.

Copyright © 2024 Ravoshia Whaley.

ISBN: 979-8224838363

Written by Ravoshia Whaley.

Origin 1993

It starts with a young married couple by the names of Sanaa and Elian Gumbs, one evening on August 1st, 1993, giving birth to a healthy baby girl in Ann Elizabeth's hospital on the island of Saint Martin. Samara weighed 6 pounds and had olive skin, brown eyes, and dark brown curly hair with a blonde patch on her left-front side.

Waah, waah, waah, (baby crying)

Nurse: "She's beautiful, what's her name?"

Sanaa: "It's Samara!"

Nurse: "She looks just like you."

Sanaa: "Thank you so much."

Out of the blue, an elderly woman with spiritual gifts enters the hospital. She walks up to the couple and baby Samara, making a stern facial expression.

Elderly Woman: "She is something special!"

Sanaa: "Aw thanks, yes, she's our special sunshine."

Elderly Woman: "Hmm well, just wait and see."

She freezes the time and puts her hand over baby Samara's head. Instantly, a silver electric spark came out of her hand.

She chants this:

"Enlighten thee with imagination at its highest,

and an unlimited flow of knowledge.

Enlighten thee!"

Sanaa and Elian leave the hospital the very next morning, bringing baby Samara home. They lived in a beautiful brick home near the beach until she was 2 years old. Unfortunately, a tragic set of events occurred in early December 1995. Such as a break-in at Elian's business office and their home set on fire.

Thankfully, Sanaa and Samara were not home at the time. And nor was Elian at the office when the break-in happened. An individual named Abu', the culprit behind both incidents, sought revenge on Elian. Because Elian had declined a partnership with him. Upon finding evidence that Abu' had committed the crimes, the police launched a search for him. But they were unsuccessful as Abu' had already fled the island.

A week later the family left the island to relocate to Washington, DC in the United States. They had two relatives who had settled there a few years prior. In no time, Elian became a success in the city with his business. While Sanaa worked at a popular hair and beauty salon.

Samara grew up full of joy as a free spirit. She didn't like the idea of following the rules at home nor school. As a result, she was often suspended and grounded for being rebellious. On the other hand, there was a particular class where Samara did pay attention and behave in, which was science. It was her favorite subject and her number one passion. She concentrated on all of the aspects, making projects and inventions.

One moment of significance, while in 8th grade, Samara presented a very interesting invention. She called it the "Mastermind Strip", which had originally been colorless. However, once she rubbed, it had enigmatically turned into the colors red, white, and black in a repeated sequence.

On the day of the presentation, the physics teacher encourages Samara to show the class her invention. Samara shrugs her shoulders and walks up to the front of the class. She is quite shy at first, talking very low. A few classmates begin to laugh at her.

Then suddenly, Samara's character and voice changes. Her teacher and classmates look in awe and confusion with their mouths wide open.

The Beginning Of The Mastermind/Lady Einstein

It's the year 2011, Samara's freshman year at Howard University in Washington, DC.

Professor Wells: "Excuse me, Miss Gumbs, this is the third time in the last two weeks that you are half an hour late."

Samara: "I'm so sorry, Professor Wells, for being late. I had an emergency."

Professor Wells: "Please see me after class."

3 Classmates: "She's such a loser." (Laughs & mocks Samara)

Samara puts her head down and whispers under her breath, seemingly annoyed by the three classmates. As the professor is lecturing, Samara's mind starts to roam with numerous letters, codes and sequences popping up. And she goes into a trance-like state. Samara imagines new methods and inventions that contribute to physics and chemistry. Additionally, Samara meets her soon to be sidekick Murray in the class. He sits right next to her and introduces himself.

Murray: "Hi, I'm Murray, what's your name?" (Smiles nervously with dimples)

Samara: "I'm Samara, it's nice to meet you." (Smiles back)

Professor Wells is lecturing and gets interrupted by Samara.

Samara: "Professor Wells, but the true essence of energy and gravity are unmeasured and unlimited, right? Imagine this..."

Samara goes into a rather lengthy dialogue explaining her point.

Professor Wells: "First you show up late, then you try to correct me. When I am certified with high honors and a part of the official committee of physics and theory. So, I have the knowledge."

Samara: "Sorry I didn't mean to impose or belittle you. I simply just wanted to inquire."

Lady Einstein/Samara: (Voice changes)

"My imagination runs wild all the time, it's a mastermind." (Mischievous laugh)

Professor Wells: "Huh, what was that? Disrupting the class won't earn you a 'A' young lady."

Nobel Prize Awards Ceremony

11 years later, Samara is a seasoned professor of physics and science at The Grand Washington University. She's also a scientist. On December 10, 2022, The Nobel Prize Awards Ceremony is presented by President Lewis and the board of committee. In addition to being honored by President Lewis, Samara wins three Nobel Prizes. One in physics, science and a special category for one of her inventions. President Lewis walks up onto the stage. The audience stands up, claps, and shouts.

President Lewis: "Ladies and gentlemen! (Crowd continues clapping) It is my pleasure and honor to announce the Nobel Prize winner for the categories Physics, Chemistry and Best New Invention to the one and only, Ms. Samara Gumbs." (Crowd cheering)

Murray: "You did it Samara! I mean Lady Einstein, go on, they're waiting for you." (Clapping & cheering)

Samara hugs her mom and dad then walks up to the podium.

Mrs. & Mr. Gumbs: "That's our baby girl yeah, woot woot!"

Samara: "I am so incredibly humbled and there's no words that can truly describe how this feels. (Teary eyes) This is a blueprint I've worked really hard on."

As I love to say: "Logic will get you from A to B. Imagination will take you everywhere."

-Albert Einstein

She unveils 2 black non-facial mannequins. One is an actual person that she turned into a mannequin using a special chemical substance. A male dancer dances around the mannequins with creativity and performance as the edgy and striking music plays.

In the presentation, her invention, called the "MPS101" (Mannequin Performance Style 101), captures kinetic energy, force, and acceleration. From a human dancing around or mimicking both mannequins in a certain way. As a result, they become in-sync as one movement.

An Interesting Flashback

A flashback of Murray and Samara/Lady Einstein in her secret laboratory with a woman and two male robbers. They are the criminal masterminds behind a popular ring of bank robberies. In the alleyway behind an Italian restaurant, Samara/Lady Einstein and Murray, along with a black Doberman Pinscher on a leash, approach three robbers.

Female Robber: "And just who are you supposed to be?"

Samara: "I'm Samara and I would like to be of assistance. I know about your robbery plans."

Female Robber: "Wait, she could be an informant for the FBI or a cop."

One Male Robber: "We're not stupid miss, plus what's up with the guard dog your fella has?"

Female Robber: "Well I am tired of being the only girl in this mix. So let's hear her out."

Samara: "I have somewhere you can hide the money."

2nd Male Robber: "Oh really... Where?"

Samara lures them into her laboratory. Once inside, Murray injects them with a sleeping drug to knock them out. About an hour later, they wake up and scream out for help. Samara mentions that nobody can hear them because it's sound proof.

Female Robber: "You lied to us girl, we shouldn't have left with you."

All Three Robbers: "Let us go please, we don't want any parts of this."

Samara: "But you think it's okay to rob so many innocent people's bank accounts. And threaten the tellers with guns, don't you? Hmm..." (Smirk smile)

She turns on a specific machine and mixes chemicals together, then pauses before going into a hypnotic state. Samara starts seeing different energy flows in the colors red, white and black. As well as, codes and equations popping up largely.

Her keen gifts become apparent as she moves around the equations and codes to arrange in the right order. Next, she completes the transformation. In consequence, the female is turned into a black non-facial mannequin, and the men turned into red ones.

(Present Time)

Samara leaves the awards ceremony. Shortly after, she arrives home and gets ready for the after-party. She puts on a jaw-dropping fitted maxi leopard print dress paired with a gold-spiked black leather jacket. Samara adds the final touches, such as red lip gloss and black gloves with red studded nails. Once finished, Samara looks in the mirror at her reflection. Then Lady Einstein, who is her, begins to speak.

Lady Einstein: (Distinctive accent) "It's okay, they've been sleeping on ya girl. I guess they didn't know you were The Mastermind/Lady Einstein. Oh, you bad girl!" (Smirks and raises her left finger to her chin)

The Show Stopper

Samara walks into the party and everyone stops and stares for a few minutes in awe. At the same time Michael Jackson's Thriller plays, making it a dramatic and cinematic entrance walk-in for her.

Lady In The Crowd: "OMG... She looks phenomenal!" (Yells out loud)

There are whispers and chatter amidst the crowd. Meanwhile, Mrs. Kensley, who is Samara's competitor, frenemy and 2x-time Nobel Prize winner, feels threatened.

Mrs. Kensley: "Hmm, whatever, she doesn't look better than me, right honey?"

Mrs. Kensley's Husband: "Of course not, not even close sweetie." (Staring intensely at Samara)

Coat Check Attendant: "Excuse me, Ms. Samara, may I take your jacket for you?"

Samara: "Yes, please thank you."

Mrs. Kensley: "Oh, I just love your dress, Samara!" (With a fake nice tone)

Samara: "Thanks, honeypie! (Dash of sarcasm) Well, I must excuse myself."

Mrs. Kensley: "Wait, let's get a picture. Baby, can you take the picture? Here's my phone."

Samara: "Um sure, but please turn on the flash."

Mrs. Kensley's Husband: "Yes, of course, no problem."

Out of the blue, a man named Ryan, who is a member of the awards committee, walks up to Samara and asks to speak to her privately. He tells her that soon after the ceremony concluded, a robbery occurred. And as a result, her metal coin plaques at the museum were stolen. In addition, two other highly valuable jewels were taken. Ryan ensures Samara that the FBI and police are on the hunt to figure out who the thieves are.

Ryan: "Is there anyone you think would deliberately do this to you? Any enemies?"

Samara: "No, not that I know of."

Ryan: "Don't worry, we will find the culprits, that's for sure. The police and FBI are investigating plus we have security footage."

Samara: "Hopefully, you do. This is awful news." (Making a disgruntled facial expression)

Ryan: "We will keep you updated."

Samara: "Okay thanks I'll appreciate that."

Samara goes back and forth angrily visualizing in her mind the thieves who stole her plaques. As she contemplates ways of revenge, Lady Einstein comes to the forefront. She excuses herself to the restroom where she is alone looking into the mirror.

Embarrassed Much

Lady Einstein: "Are you freaking kidding me! (Slams hands down onto the counter) Samara let's show them who they're messing with."

Samara: "Hold on, we don't want to blow things up or go too far. And let's keep it cute at this event, please. Later we'll go into full effect."

Lady Einstein: "Ugh, you're such a softy, why not? Let's have some real fun, after all, this is your night. Oh, and Mrs. Kensley deserves a lesson taught after what she did. She thinks you don't have the slightest idea." (Smirks)

Referring to the fact that, before Samara received the news about winning the three Nobel Prizes, Mrs. Kensley tried to bribe committee members to award her instead, which is prohibited.

Samara: "Ah, I know that girl is so fake she can't fool me or anyone with real intelligence."

Lady Einstein: "She'll see tonight that she can't cross us and get away with it."

Samara: "Alright, we'll have some fun just a little though."

Woman In Restroom Stall: "Cough, Cough!" (Listening the whole time)

The entire time Samara is talking to Lady Einstein (herself) in the mirror, a woman in a restroom stall is listening. At one point, she looks under the stall to see who Samara is speaking to but notices she is talking to herself. The woman only sees Samara (Lady Einstein) at the counter in front of the mirror. Stunned because she thought it was two people having a conversation. Once Samara hears the coughs and the toilet flush, she rushes out of the bathroom feeling embarrassed.

Woman In Restroom Stall: "Hack, ahem, ahem... (Toilet flushing) Gosh, what a real weirdo!"

Samara re-enters the party heading over to the appetizer section to grab a few mini burgers and chocolate-covered strawberries. Jenn, Samara's best friend, sees her walking and yells out "Ayee sexy lady". Samara smiles and goes to Jenn, and they sit down at the bar. Soon after, Jenn spots Samara's boy toy (friend with benefits) named Malcolm.

Jenn: "Hey, isn't that your loverboy or should I say boy toy hehe?"

Samara: "Yeah, and he looks good in his outfit tonight yum looking like a snack."

Jenn: "More like dinner ha!" (Laughs)

Samara: "I know that he sees me. He just wants me to go over to him."

Jenn: "Ahh, nope he's walking over to us now."

Malcolm: "Hi beautiful! (Smiles at Samara) What's up, Jenn?!" (Makes annoyed facial expression)

Samara: "Hey there handsome." (Blushing)

Malcolm: "Let me get another peach Moscato for the lady."

Jenn: "Umm, what about me huh, am I invisible?" (Rolls eyes)

Malcolm: "And another of whatever she's drinking sir."

Bartender: "Alright coming right up!"

Dance Battle

Samara flirts and talks with Malcolm for a while. Malcolm congratulates her for winning the three Nobel Prizes. He also kisses her on the cheek and pulls her waist closer to him. After that, they go to the dance floor and begin dancing. But just as the two are about to kiss, it's interrupted when Mrs. Kensley dances, trying to outshine Samara. Then Samara gives Mrs. Kensley an intense glare, which stirs up quite a dramatic scene. The crowd makes a circle around them and begins to chant "Dance battle". As a result, they start the battle by dancing to Super Freaky Girl by Nicki Minaj.

DJ: "Ladies and gentlemen, we seem to have a dance battle brewing here. Might I add we have the one and only, our latest Nobel Prize winner Ms. Samara. (Crowd cheers) And the spicy two-time winner Mrs. Kensley." (Crowd surrounds Samara and Mrs. Kensley)

Samara: "Please, she can't see me on the dance floor or in Physics."

Mrs. Kensley: "Prove it then Samara!" (Bring it on hand gesture)

The dance battle starts with round one as Samara and Mrs. Kensley each go back and forth. Samara wins the 1st round judged by the crowd's cheers. But for the second round, Mrs. Kensley takes it. Once the third round begins Lady Einstein strikes. She purposely gets close to Mrs. Kensley and then steps very hard on her right foot for a few seconds.

Ironically, the crowd doesn't notice it. Mrs. Kensley bends down low to grab her foot, screaming out in pain. While Lady Einstein whispers into her ear pretending to help her.

Mrs. Kensley: "Ouch, ouch, my foot hurts so bad!"

She makes whimpering noises while bending down to grab her foot.

Lady Einstein: "Who do you think you are messing with? If I were you I would steer clear. I am the only mastermind around here. You're just an imposter, a wannabe."

Mrs. Kensley: "Honey, I need your help please." (Limping away with her husband assisting)

DJ: "And... the winner is Ms. Samara."

(Crowd screams)

Mrs. Kensley: "Cheater humph!" (Yells)

Malcolm: "Welp, you showed her sick dance moves by the way. I didn't know you could move that way."

Samara/Lady Einstein: "Some things are quite mysterious, including me."

Quote:

"Lady Einstein is quite mischievous, a little mysterious, brilliant and likes to play."

-The Mastermind/Lady Einstein

Stalker Alert

After the brutal dance battle, Samara leaves the party with Jenn and tells Malcolm she will see him later at her place. Once they arrive at Samara's condo, a strange and suspicious male in all black watches them. He secretly snaps pictures while sitting in a blue Toyota with dark-tinted windows. The guy seemed to have been following Samara and Jenn from the party.

In actuality, the man is a private investigator hired by someone to keep tabs on Samara. Jenn stays over for a little while, then leaves. But as she walks towards her car she hears someone creeping behind her. She becomes frazzled and rushes into her car. Jenn drives off slowly, catching a good glimpse of the strange man. In the blink of an eye, the man runs across behind her car and she sees him from the rearview mirror. Freaking out, Jenn immediately calls Samara to warn her about it.

(Samara's cell phone rings)

Samara: "Hello, hey girl what's up? Did you forget something?"

Jenn: "No, but I'm a little freaked out. I saw a man following behind me while walking to my car."

Samara: "Seriously, are you okay?"

Jenn: "Yes, and to be honest, it seems like he'd been watching us for a while, or perhaps just keeping an eye on you. Once I drove off, I could see him standing behind the side of a blue car. He was staring up at your living room window as I drove by."

Samara: "Hmm, oh really now. So I have a stalker on my hands." (Looks outside of her window)

Jenn warned Samara to be careful, seemingly worried about her safety. She also told her that protection of some kind is necessary. Afterward, Samara (apparently taking Jenn's advice) searches for her taser and pepper spray. As well as she grabs a knife from the kitchen and hides it under the bed just in case.

Lady Einstein (Samara) starts thinking about

different ways to punish the supposed stalker if she were to catch him. At that moment, she hears a text message notification. It is Malcolm asking her if he can come over now. Samara responds with "Yes honey, come now" (with a kissing emoji). He texts back "Okay be there in a few" (wink emoji). She then gets in the shower and slips on a sexy Victoria's Secret red two-piece lingerie with a matching silk robe.

Subsequently, the doorbell rings and Samara opens the door, smiling at Malcolm. She raises her finger in a sexy manner telling him to come in. He grabs and kisses her while going inside. Samara gets the strawberries and chocolate from the kitchen counter and takes them into the bedroom. (Dramatic moment as Play-N-Skillz "Freaks" starts playing)

Samara and Malcolm feed strawberries and chocolate to each other, ultimately spending a passionate night together. Upon waking up in the morning, Samara rushes him out and mentions that she's late for a meeting. She then throws his clothes at him.

Samara: "Crap I'm going to be late. I need you to go."

Malcolm: "Wait, don't I get a hug and kiss goodbye? (Seemingly offended) You try to come off tough like you don't have a heart. But deep down I know you care. I'll see you around, bye."

Meeting Dr. Maxwell

Three months later "Spring 2023", Samara enters Empire Mall for some shopping. But she decides to stop by the food court first. In the meantime, a tall man with gray hair approaches her.

Dr. Maxwell: "If it's not the beautiful genius herself, my goodness!"

Samara: "Do I know you?"

Dr. Maxwell: "No, not personally, but you may have heard of me."

Samara: "Enlighten me then!"

He reaches to shake her hand and says "I'm Dr. Maxwell Livingstone".

Samara: "Wow, I've heard of you, this is such an honor, sir."

Dr. Maxwell: "Do you have a few minutes to spare? I would love to join you for lunch."

Samara: "Of course, first, let me order here at Luke's Fried Chicken. And I'll meet you at that table right over there." (Points to the table)

The two speak for an hour discussing various ideas. Dr. Maxwell convinces Samara to partner up with him for a specific new project he's working on. She is also invited to Livingstone's World Of Science and Technology. Lady Einstein takes over for a split second, as Samara pauses.

Lady Einstein: "No, don't do it! We don't need him, Samara. Dr. Maxwell isn't any better than you and he just wants to use you. Something feels fishy, I don't trust him."

Samara: "Umm, please stop! I think this is a great opportunity. He's a legend after all."

Dr. Maxwell: "Samara hello, is everything okay?" (Waves his hand in front of her face)

Samara accepts his invitation, unaware of his plan. Dr. Maxwell plans on tricking Samara (Lady Einstein) into giving him her secret formulas and methods. Upon the first day of her arrival, Dr. Maxwell's assistant shows her around the facility. At the end of the tour, Samara receives a phone call from Murray. He expresses his concerns and suspicions about Dr. Maxwell. Samara reassures him that all is well. On the contrary, Murray tells her that she doesn't even know him. He points out rumors about Dr. Maxwell's crooked and backstabbing ways.

Before hanging up the phone, Samara encouraged him to come visit the lab. The following day, he agrees to meet with Dr. Maxwell and Samara. However, Dr. Maxwell deliberately excludes Murray once he's there. He implies that what he and Samara are working on cannot be shared with him. Just before Murray leaves the laboratory, he pulls Samara to the side alone to warn her to watch out. Because he is not convinced and doesn't trust Dr. Maxwell.

Samara screams at Murray and tells him to get out of here and that he's just jealous. As a consequence, Murray was left in a state of distraught. Multiple weeks pass by while she steadily works with Dr. Maxwell. He earns Samara's trust significantly, which puts a strain on her and Murray. One evening, Dr. Maxwell announces a big event where he will unveil the new invention that he and Samara have been working on. Thrilled with excitement, Samara calls Murray to invite him, but he doesn't pick up so she just leaves a voicemail.

The Betrayal

On the day of the event, Samara was extremely pumped and eager to present the invention that she and Dr. Maxwell worked on. But unfortunately, he's got something else in mind.

Samara: "I can't wait till we show them what we have created. I'm so excited."

Dr. Maxwell: "Uh, you mean my creation?" (With a menacing look in his eyes)

Samara: (In disbelief) "But, I thought we were in this together."

Realizing he has tricked her, she re-plays the moments when she first met him. Samara gets flashbacks and looks to see what she may have missed, that were red flags.

Lady Einstein: "I knew it, I told you he was no good."

Samara: "Yes you did, I should have listened."

Dr. Maxwell: (Ominous type of laugh) "Who are you talking to young lady?"

Samara: "Wait a minute it was you the whole time. You had some stalker guy watching and following me, right? My friend saw him one night, you bastard. How much did you pay the creep to spy on me?"

Dr. Maxwell: "I don't know what you're talking about." (Smirks)

Lady Einstein: "You'll regret this!"

Just as she reaches for an injection needle, he quickly hits her from behind with a wooden vase.

Dr. Maxwell: "Not so fast, haha."

Two hours before the event, Dr. Maxwell drugs and ties Samara up. He leaves her trapped in the basement. While in solitude, she has flashbacks and memories of Murray, her right hand and whom she's always trusted. Samara regrets not believing him. Despite this, Murray appears out of nowhere and unties Samara.

Samara: "Thank you so much for rescuing me, Murray. (Hugs him) I'm sorry that I didn't trust you. Can you forgive me?"

Murray is filled with a warm fuzzy feeling of gratitude.

Murray: "It's okay, I forgive you. I'll always be here no matter what till the wheels fall off, Samara." (Gazing into her eyes)

Samara: (Smiles while hugging Murray) "Now we need a plan because he thinks he's won. But I can't allow that to happen."

They're quick to come up with a plan. Samara calls Jenn and a man named Lavett, who is a well-trained fighter, to help distract as well as fight off the security guards. Next, she proceeds toward the very thing that will embarrass Dr. Maxwell and give her both revenge and justice.

Shortly after Jenn arrives, she wanders off from the crowd onto a lower floor. Two security guards approach her, asking if she is lost. At this exact moment, Jenn collapses to the ground and screams out loud, causing quite a commotion.

Jenn: (Screams in anguish) "Omg it hurts so bad! Someone, please help me."

The two guards assist Jenn. Simultaneously, Samara sneaks past and enters laboratory 0012 to get the missing component she hid from Dr. Maxwell.

Jenn: "Oops, sorry. (Raises from the ground) It must have been some extreme gas or acid reflux. I feel better now!"

2 Security Guards: "Ma'am, you have to be escorted back to the presentation now."

They take Jenn back to the main event. Whilst, Lavett fights off five other security guards on another floor. Murray makes his way into the sound check stage DJ section. Once there, he injects the two sound-check men with a temporary sleeping drug. Therefore, he'll be in control of the microphones and sound system. Murray provides Samara with an additional microphone, to complete their plan of exposing Dr. Maxwell.

Sike Gotcha

D r. Maxwell is announced to the stage by the presenters. He receives a standing ovation and proceeds to unveil the invention.

Dr. Maxwell: "Hello everyone, get ready for something extraordinary, brilliant and mind-blowing. This is a real game-changer here folks! I present to you "The Energy Einsteiner 555"."

He claims that it is a powerful force of nature. A machine that transfers pure kinetic energy into the hands and fingers. But it's not visible to the naked eye. It can only be seen with a red, white and black striped patch that is put on the right hand of each attendee.

Dr. Maxwell begins to demonstrate the invention. All seems to be going well until it stops working halfway through. He stops at this moment and wonders why things aren't going the way they're supposed to. Suddenly, Lady Einstein (Samara) appears from the audience with a microphone.

Lady Einstein: "Well, well, ladies and gentlemen Dr. Maxwell appears to have a problem, won't you agree? But don't worry, I can be of assistance. After all, this is my design and invention that he is claiming." (Laughs while walking up on stage)

Dr. Maxwell: "Security, get this woman off this stage. She's a liar!"

Lady Einstein: "See you're missing the most intricate piece of the puzzle here for this design." (Holds up the missing piece)

(The audience gasps as she whispers to him)

Lady Einstein: "Deep down, I had a slight suspicion that you would play me. So before you revealed your true intentions and kidnapped me, I removed the one key piece needed for the invention."

Flashback

The day before the big event, Samara (Lady Einstein) takes the specific piece and hides it. While Dr. Maxwell steps out of the laboratory.

Dr. Maxwell: (Whispers in her ear) "They won't believe you, silly woman!"

Samara/Lady Einstein: (Turns to audience)

"This imposter knocked me out, and locked me away in the basement. He basically kidnapped me."

(Audience gasps)

The police arrive and cuff Dr. Maxwell right in front of everyone.

Dr. Maxwell: "This isn't over, Samara!"

Samara/Lady Einstein: "It's Lady Einstein to you and never forget it." (Gives him the middle finger discreetly)

Lady Einstein (Samara) receives a standing ovation and a round of applause from everyone. At the same time, Dr. Maxwell gets taken away in handcuffs.

She tells the audience:

"Sometimes in life the biggest mysteries are the secrets to one's own potential of achieving greatness."

Murray claps and smiles at Samara (Lady Einstein), as she winks at him while her tongue touches her top teeth. She walks out of the event

with paparazzi and reporters following behind.

Paparazzi & Reporters: "Samara, Lady Einstein, please look this way. Is it true that Dr. Maxwell kidnapped you and tried to steal your work?"

Samara/Lady Einstein: "Yes, indeed!"

(Cameras flashing)

An FBI Agent named Leroy Grant briefly speaks with Samara, informing her that Dr. Maxwell was under investigation for something similar. He's also grateful to have caught him in the act.

Leroy Grant: "Thank you so much, Samara. We've been keeping a close eye on Dr. Maxwell for some time now. But we didn't have enough to pin him down until now."

Samara/Lady Einstein: "No problem, I'm at your service, sir."

San Francisco, California Year 2025

(In San Francisco, California)

Joseph: "Hello... Hello!" (Waiting)

Assistant: "Hello, how may I help you, sir?"

Joseph: "Hi, I would like to speak to The Mastermind at Masterminds Inc."

Assistant: "Well, I'm sorry to say, but The Mastermind isn't taking any new appointments at this time."

Joseph: "Oh why not? I need help with something urgent. And I know they can provide the necessary resources. Some important people are depending on me to get The Mastermind on board."

Assistant: "And what is your name?"

Joseph: "It's Joseph Hudson."

Assistant: "Give me a moment, hold please."

(Connected)

The Mastermind/Lady Einstein: "Hello, this is The Mastermind. What is it that you are seeking, Mr. Joseph?" She uses a voice machine to disguise her real voice.

Joseph: "Can we meet soon? I need to speak with you in person."

The Mastermind/Lady Einstein: "Okay, tomorrow at 3 pm sharp, and don't be late."

Joseph enters Masterminds Inc., a large red, white and black building with a waterfall in front of it. In addition, there are five Doberman Pinschers on leashes held by men in suits.

Once inside, he walks over to the front desk receptionist and tells her that he's there for an appointment. The receptionist takes him to The Mastermind's office and he waits a few minutes in anticipation. Instantaneously, it's revealed that "The Mastermind" is a woman.

She turns around in her chair (dramatic slow motion) wearing a studded red, white and black leather jacket and says: "Hello, I'm The Mastermind/Lady Einstein"! (In a distinctive tone)

Lastly, she does a side-smirk-like smile with her left index finger on her chin. Quote:

"I always have a masterplan on my mind, it never ends."

-The Mastermind/Lady Einstein